P U B L I S H I N G

P.O. BOX 1214 PAHOA, HAWAII 96778
PHONE and FAX: (808) 965-6443
EMAIL: kenkudo@starlei.com

ISBN 0-9748412-0-X

First Edition, First Printing – 2004

The Littlest Pahoehoe

By Ken Kudo

Illustrated By Fil Kearney

The Littlest Pahoehoe 3d face created by Aran Graham

StarLei

To Keicy, my littlest pahoehoe

Long Ago, in old hawaii, in a place where volcanoes erupted and land met the sea, out of the fire of hot flowing lava came very many Pahoehoe (*pa-hoy-hoy*) lava rocks. The smooth, dark rocks laid along the shore and they were of different sizes and shapes. Some were big, some were flat, and some were long. There was also something very special about these rocks.

They all had Mana - - the fire of life.

Among them was the littlest *Pahoehoe* lava rock. The other rocks teased him for being so little. It made him very sad.

"Hey, little Opai (*oh- pie*) shrimp! Move over, small Pipipi (*pee- pee- pee*) snail!" they said. He wished for magic words to help him. Everyday, he made up new words but the teasing didn't stop and he continued to be sad.

6

Then one day he said some different magic words. The teasing didn't stop, but he wasn't sad anymore. They were new and strange words, and made no sense to him. But everytime he said the words, "Rock 'n Roll", he felt strong and happy.

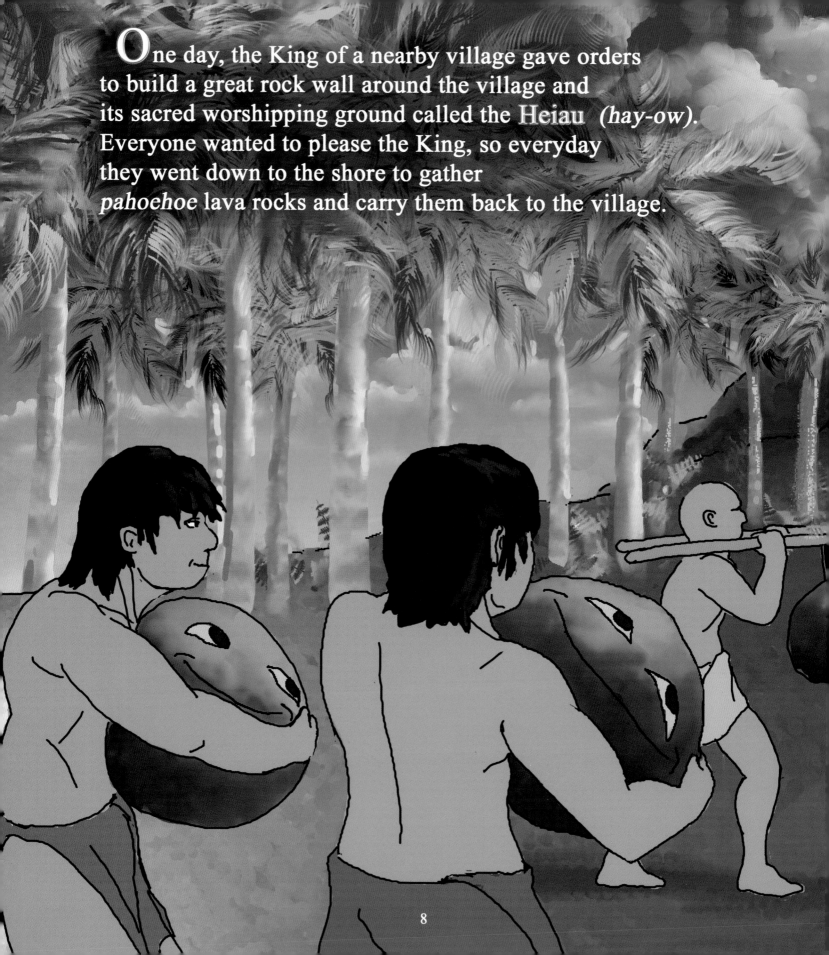

One day, the King of a nearby village gave orders
to build a great rock wall around the village and
its sacred worshipping ground called the Heiau *(hay-ow)*.
Everyone wanted to please the King, so everyday
they went down to the shore to gather
pahoehoe lava rocks and carry them back to the village.

The rocks were proud and happy. To be chosen for the King's wall made them feel like *Alii* (ah-lee-ee) [royalty].

9

But the littlest pahoehoe was too little to be chosen for the King's wall. Soon, all the other lava rocks were gone, and the little pahoehoe was the only rock left on the shore. He felt sad and alone. But then, he remembered his magic words.

Rock 'n Roll!" he shouted.

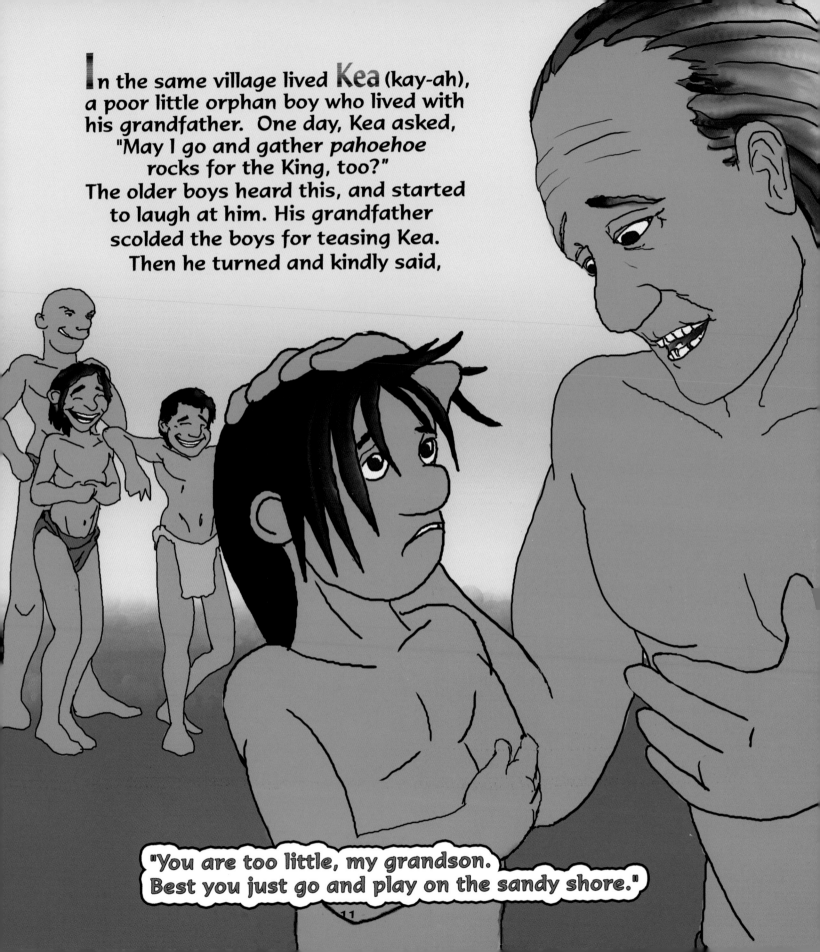

In the same village lived **Kea** (kay-ah),
a poor little orphan boy who lived with
his grandfather. One day, Kea asked,
"May I go and gather *pahoehoe*
rocks for the King, too?"
The older boys heard this, and started
to laugh at him. His grandfather
scolded the boys for teasing Kea.
Then he turned and kindly said,

"You are too little, my grandson.
Best you just go and play on the sandy shore."

11

Kea obeyed his grandfather and went to the shore, but he didn't feel like playing. He wanted to help the King and felt sad for being teased by the bigger boys. Then he saw the littlest *pahoehoe* and picked him up.

"I'm not too little," Kea said to the rock. "Watch me toss you high into the sky, and onto the wings of that *Iiwi* (ee-vee) bird!"

12

With one great sweep of his arm, Kea threw the little pahoehoe as high as the brightly colored *Iiwi* flew.

"Rock 'n Rollllll!!" screamed the little pahoehoe, as he flew through the air.

Thump! The little rock landed on the bird's back.

"Hold on tight!" said playful *Iiwi*.

"I cannot!" yelled back little *pahoehoe*, trying to keep his balance.

After a very short ride,
the rock rolled off the
wings of *Iiwi*

A nd, "Clunk!"
landed on the edge of the rain forest below among the
mean and angry A'a *(ah-ah)* lava rocks hiding under the
vines. They were not as smooth and round as little *pahoehoe*.

"Go Away!"

"Get Lost!"

yelled
the jagged,
rough a'a .

The littlest *pahoehoe*
felt frightened and lost.
Then he remembered his
magic words and felt strong.

"Rock 'n Roll!" he shouted.

Suddenly a loud voice screamed, "Quiet! Naughty *a'a*! Shame on you!"

It was **Hapuu** *(ha-pooh)*, the giant tree fern of the forest.

The *a'a* stopped.

"Don't be afraid, little *pahoehoe*, the *a'a* are friendly once you get to know them," said *Hapuu*.

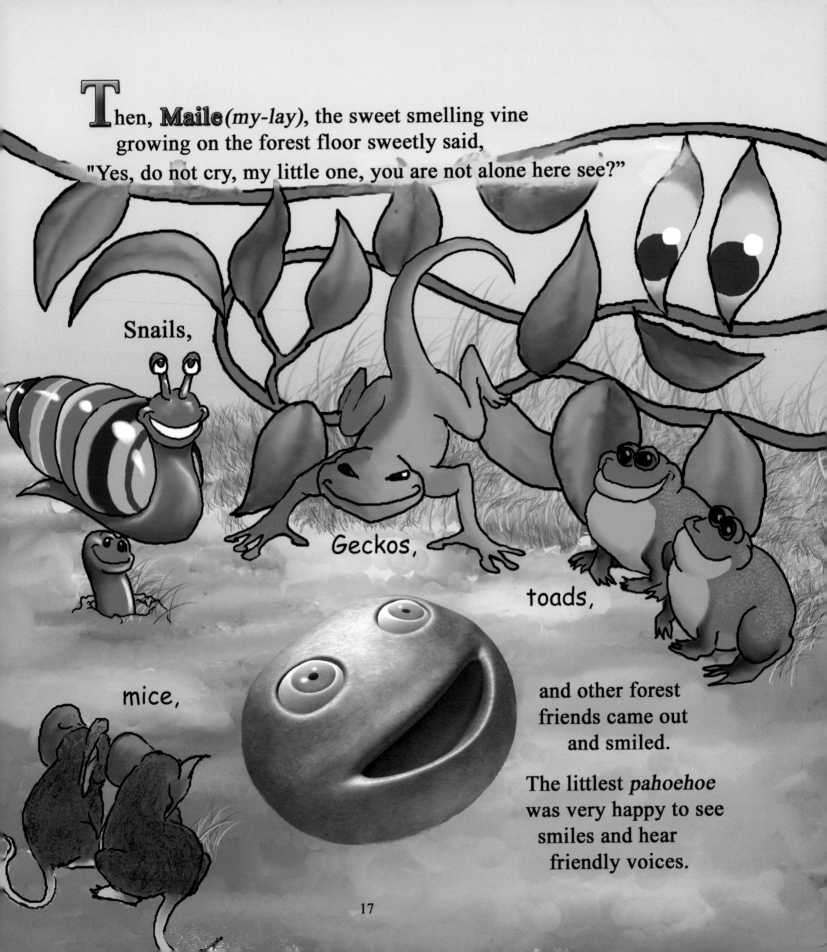

Then, **Maile** *(my-lay)*, the sweet smelling vine
growing on the forest floor sweetly said,
"Yes, do not cry, my little one, you are not alone here see?"

Snails,

Geckos,

toads,

mice,

and other forest
friends came out
and smiled.

The littlest *pahoehoe*
was very happy to see
smiles and hear
friendly voices.

17

Then happy *Iiwi* began to sing a happy song. *Hapuu, Maile,* and the other friends of the forest all joined in. With all the music and laughter, little *pahoehoe* and the *a'a* started to jiggle and move. It made everyone happy.

"Now that's Rock 'n Roll!" They all laughed.

(Everyone sing along and dance the 'jungle jiggle')

JUNGLE PALS
(Sung to the tune of Jingle Bells)

Chorus:
Jungle Pals, Jungle Pals, Jungles all the way,
Friends forever, here together, happy come what may, oh,
Jungle Pals, Jungle Pals, Jungles all the way,
Oh how merry we can be on a rainy forest day

Verse 1:
Lying in the mud, at *Po-ho-iki Bay*
In the rain we grow, laughing all the way
Big mosquitoes bite, makes us feel alright
Oh, how happy we can be with forest friends tonight, oh,
repeat Chorus

Verse 2:
We don't have bills or rents, we love our leaky tents
We're happy in the cold, and even where there's mold,
Our neighbors are not rude, and we have lots of food
Living in a neighborhood with a cheerful, happy mood, oh,

repeat Chorus

Verse 3:
We love to sing and dance, and play with all the ants
Our neighbors are good bugs, and happy friendly slugs.
We're friends with all the trees, the birds, and all the bees,
All we ever really want is just to stay here please, oh.

repeat Chorus

Oh, how merry we can be on a rainy forest day.

onths later, not far away, the great royal rock wall was almost pau (*pow*) [finished]. And what a great royal wall it was-- the largest in the land.

Never was there a more solid and beautiful wall.

Never was there a finer selection of *pahoehoe* lava rocks.

The King seemed pleased, but as he admired the great entrance pillar, he suddenly stopped.

20

"Auwe!" (*away*) he shouted.
Everyone looked. At the top
front of the great pillar, there
was a tiny empty space.
The empty spot made the
pillar look very bad.

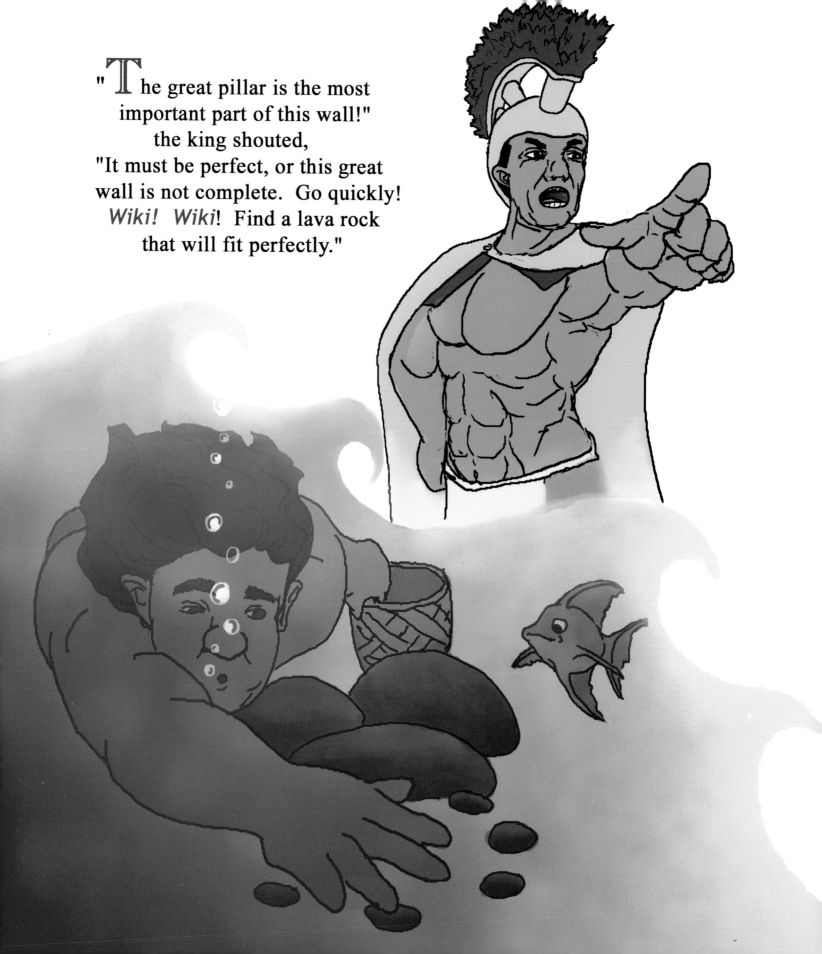

"The great pillar is the most important part of this wall!" the king shouted, "It must be perfect, or this great wall is not complete. Go quickly! *Wiki! Wiki*! Find a lava rock that will fit perfectly."

Everyone began searching.
Day and night they searched,

high and low they searched.
They searched near and far.

They searched on land
and in the sea,
on mountains and streams,

but no one could find
the right pahoehoe
lava rock.

23

Some rocks
were too big,
some rocks
were too fat,

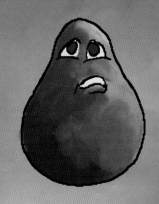

Some were too pointed,
some were too flat.

Some rocks had cracks,
some were too long,

Some were
    too slippery,
some were not strong.

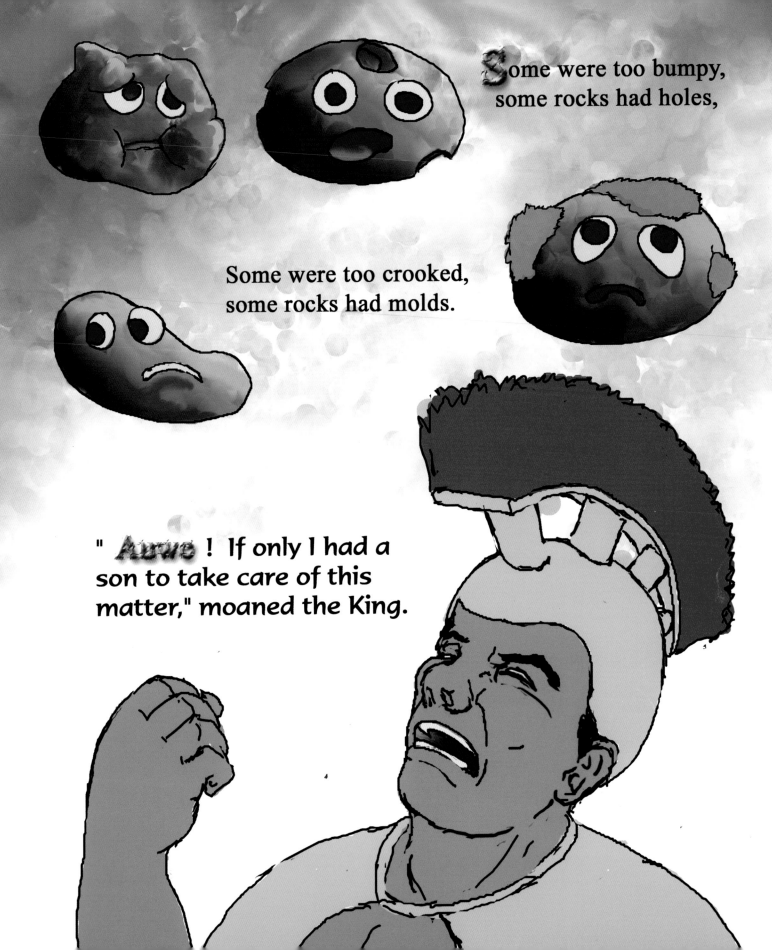

Some were too bumpy, some rocks had holes,

Some were too crooked, some rocks had molds.

" Auwe ! If only I had a son to take care of this matter," moaned the King.

Flying high overhead, *Iiwi* flew back to his forest friends with the exciting news.

"Wow!" shouted the little *pahoehoe*,
"If only I could be chosen for the king's wall-- but who
will ever find me here in this forest?"
Everyone became quiet and started thinking.

Then suddenly
Iiwi shouted,

"Look, its Kea
playing by the ocean!!"

"I have an idea!" said *Maile*.
She whispered her plan
and they all
all got excited.

"What are we
waiting for?
Lets Rock 'n Roll!"
They shouted.

27

Iiwi flew low on the surf and called to Kea, then flew in circles on the sand. Kea playfully chased him round and round.

Then, *Iiwi* flew up and down the beach,
and Kea chased him up and down the beach.

Then *Iiwi* flew into the edge of the forest and Kea followed. Soon the boy was tired from the chase and the sun's heat. That's when *Hapuu* spread her shady fronds.

"Ahhh Yes! A cool place to rest," Kea thought. He snuggled under her fronds. As he rested, *Maile* released her fragrance. It made the forest air smell sweet.

"Ahhhhh, the smell of sweet *maile*", thought Kea. It reminded him of his sweet mother. Kea became relaxed and laid down close to the sweet smelling vines. He almost fell asleep when he heard a tiny voice saying, "Rock 'n Roll!"

"Rock and Roll?" said Kea. No sooner he said that, Kea noticed that he felt different. He wasn't sad anymore for being teased, and he felt strong and happy.

Then he spied the littlest *pahoehoe* peeking out behind *Maile*. Kea's eyes gleamed.

"This is the rock the King needs! I just know it!" he joyfully shouted.

Kea ran back to his village as fast as he could clutching the littlest *pahoehoe* in his fist.

Standing at his pillar, the King's eyes opened wide as brave little Kea approached with his rock. "What have we here?" said the King, examining the little *pahoehoe*.

He placed it on the pillar …carefully. Then he stepped back to look.

Then he stepped forward and looked.

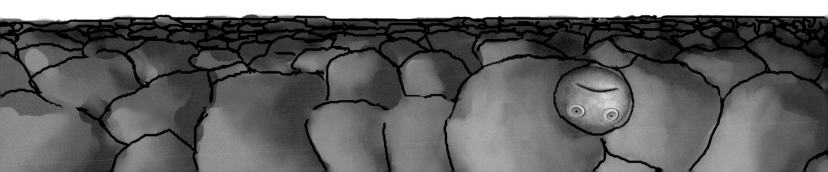

Then he stepped to the side and looked.

He even stepped on top of the pillar and looked.

By then, the whole village had gathered to look, including Kea's grandfather and all the older boys.

"Its Perfect!!"
the King finally said. Then he turned to the crowd and spoke,
"We have been working so hard that we had forgotten how much we need our little children, like Kea and his littlest *pahoehoe*. Because of them, this great rockwall is finally *pau*! In order for us not to forget this important lesson, from this day forth, you will honor Kea as my Hanai (*hun-eye*) son and he will be the royal keeper of this great wall. Mahalo !"

34

The villagers cheered and celebrated as the gracious King hugged and lifted his happy adopted son.

"Rock 'n Roll!!!!!!!" Kea shouted to the crowd at the top of his lungs.

Many sweet *Maile* and lovely *Hapuu* were planted along the sacred *Heiau* and royal rockwall. Flocks of *Iiwi* and other forest friends came everyday to sing and play.

nd the littlest pahoehoe was the happiest royal rock on the tallest and most important pillar in all of Hawaii. And from that day forth, he never used his magic words, for there was never a lava rock large or small, on land or in the sea, that would ever tease or laugh at him again.

The End

Glossary *

Pahoehoe *(pahoyhoy)*	Very hot lava which flows forward. Pahoehoe rocks are heavy and solid - smooth and rounded on the shore by sand and wave action.
A'a *(uh-uh)*	A'a lava rocks are brittle, jagged lava rocks, formed by a'a lava that crumble, rather than flow forward.
Hanai *(huh-nye)*	Adopted.
Heiau *(hay-ow)*	Sacred ancient Hawaiian worshipping ground.
Iiwi *(ee-vee)*	Indigenous colorful Hawaiian birds with long, curved beaks.
Hapuu *(huh-poo)*	Tree Ferns indigenous to Hawaii
Maile *(my-lay)*	Fragrant vines used for leis.
Pau *(pow)*	Finished, the end.
Auwe *(ah-way)*	Aw Shucks
Opai (Oh-pie)	Small shrimp
Pipipi (Pee-pee-pee)	Small black shoreline snail
Mana (Ma-Nuh)	The Life force within all things
Mahalo (Muh-huh-low)	Thank you
Wiki Wiki (Weeky-weeky)	Hurry up, be quick.

* Practical pronunciations

39